Why Do I Have to Make My Bed?

OR, A HISTORY OF MESSY ROOMS

by Wade Bradford + Illustrations by Johanna van der Sterre

TRICYCLE PRESS
BERKELEY

"Why do I have to make my bed?" I said.

"I already put the dishes in the dishwasher. I dusted off my video games. I even picked up my dinosaurs, my racetrack, and my robot-monkey action figures. So why do I have to make my bed? It's just going to get messed up again."

Mom raised her eyebrow and said, "That reminds me of a story about your grandmother, when she was a little girl. And that little girl was as grumpy as a groundhog, and she said, 'I already washed and dried the dishes. I dusted my rock'n'roll records. I even picked up my slinky, my Hula-hoops, and my roller skates. Gee whiz, why do I have to make my bed?'

Her mother just tapped her foot and said, 'That reminds me of a story about your grandfather, when he was a little boy. And that little boy was as mad as a wet cat, and he said . . .

'I already fetched water from the pump. I dusted the phonograph. I even picked up my spinning tops, my toy train, and my tin soldiers. Pray tell, Mother, why do I have to make my bed?'

1911

His mother just smirked and said, 'That reminds me of a story about your great-grandmother, when she was a little girl. And that little girl was as bothersome as a badger, and she said . . .

'I already drew water from the well. I dusted off Pa's fiddle. I even picked up my lasso, my marbles, and my rag dolly. Land's sakes, Ma, why do I have to make my bed?'

Her mother just scrubbed the table and said, 'That reminds me of a story about your great-grandfather, when he was a little boy. And that little boy was as ruffled as a hen, and he said . . .

1801

'I already hung my britches to dry. I dusted Father's printing press. I even picked up the eggs in the henhouse and the tomatoes in the garden. So why do I have to make my bed?'

His mother just fluttered her fan and said, 'That reminds me of a story about your great-great-great-grandmother, when she was a little girl. And that little girl was as cantankerous as an old sea dog, and she said . . .

1762

'I already swabbed the deck. I dusted off the captain's spy scope. I even picked out the rats that were hiding in the pickle barrel. So why do I have to make my bed?'

Her mother just clucked her tongue and said, 'That reminds me of a story about your double-great-great-great-grandfather, when he was a little boy. And that little boy was as wicked as a warlock, and he said . . .

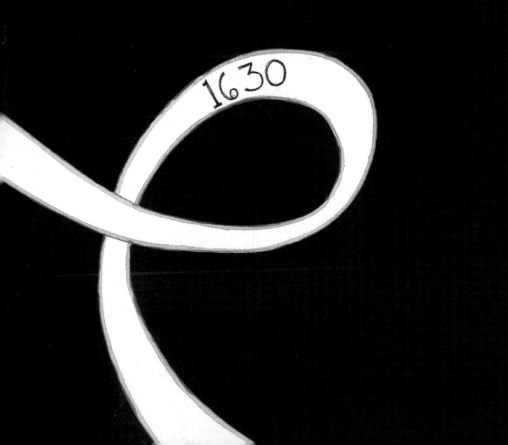

1630

'I already sheared the sheep and milked the yak. I dusted off Sister's loom. I even picked up the pig droppings and planted the wheat. So why do I have to make my bed?'

His mother just put her hands on her hips and said, 'That reminds me of a story about your double-great-great-double-double-great-great-grandmother, when she was a little girl. And that little girl was more thunderous than Thor, and she said . . .

'I already stoked the fire for the sword maker. I dusted off the sacred blowing horn. I even picked up the broken spears and patched up Father's war wounds. So why do I have to make my bed?'

Her mother just burped and said, 'That reminds me of
a story about your triple-great-triple-great-great-
grandfather, when he was a little boy. And that
little boy was as ill-tempered as a caged lion,
and he said . . .

'I already unclogged the aqueducts. I dusted off the statues. I even picked up after the gladiators. So why do I have to make my bed?'

His mother just brushed her golden hair and said, 'That reminds me of a story about your triple-great-great-triple-triple-great-great-great-grandmother, when she was a little girl. And that little girl was as cranky as a crocodile, and she said . . .

'I already gave water to the pyramid builders. I dusted off Father's papyrus scrolls. I even gathered up the plague of frogs Big Brother snuck into our tent. So why do I have to make my bed?'

Her mother brushed a frog off her tunic and said, 'That reminds me of a story about one of your ancestors, when he was a little boy. And that little boy was as sour as a saber-toothed tiger, and he said . . .

'Me already clean cave! Me hunt mammoth! Me dust stalagmites. Me make fire! Why me have to make bed? It just get messed up again!'

'Why!

Why!

Why!'

His mother just stared at him and said, 'Because I said so.'

'Oh,' said the cave boy, who then straightened his bed of sticks and furs.

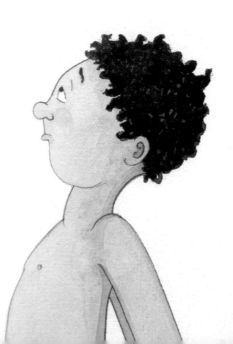

'Oh,' said the Egyptian girl, who fluffed up her bed of flax and linen.

'Oh,' said the Roman boy, who smoothed the wrinkles out of his wool blanket.

'Oh,' said the Viking girl, who shook the fleas from her caribou hide.

'Oh,' said the Norman boy, who stuffed more goose feathers into his pillow.

'Oh,' said the pilgrim girl, who neatly folded her mother's quilt.

'Oh,' said the Virginian boy, who pulled up his sheets nice and straight.

'Oh,' said the country girl, who heaped handfuls of hay into her mattress.

'Oh,' said the city boy, who tucked his sheets under the corners.

'Oh,' said your grandmother, who made everything tidy and neat.

"And that," Mom said as she lowered her raised eyebrow, "is the end of the story."

"Oh," I said.

And then, I made my bed.

Chores Through the Ages

40,000 BC – 10,000 BC: Prehistoric Times

Children of the Stone Age probably spent much of their time learning survival skills from their family members. They learned how to hunt, how to tell the difference between nutritious plants and poisonous ones, how to build shelters, and how to carve, smooth, and sharpen basic tools.

So what did they do for fun? Archaeologists have discovered doll-like figurines that Stone Age children might have played with. Evidence also suggests that children would sometimes paint Paleolithic art on cave walls, right alongside their parents' artwork. Families during the Stone Age domesticated dogs as far back as 30,000 BC, so there's a good chance that prehistoric children played the game of fetch, just like kids do today.

1000 BC: Ancient Egypt

Girls in ancient Egypt helped their mothers prepare food and grow plants from herb gardens for spices and medicine. Boys were often in charge of watching the livestock. They would lead cattle through the fields. The animals' hooves would squish seeds of grain deep into the earth, helping to plant crops. One of the smelliest chores for Egyptian children involved collecting dried cattle droppings, an excellent fuel for fire.

But Egyptian life wasn't all dried poop. Children played with toy animals made from baked clay. They also built toy boats to sail along the irrigation canals.

121 AD: The Roman Empire

For children in ancient Rome, their level of education depended upon their family's status. Wealthy families could afford to educate their children in schools. Boys learned how to read and write in Latin. They often learned mathematics, science, speech-making, and combat. Girls learned about sewing, spinning, and other household chores.

Roman children enjoyed a game known as Trochus. To play, kids rolled a large metal hoop, hitting it with a stick to see how long they could keep it moving. They also played a popular game called Terni Lapilli. (You have probably played this game, too. Today it's known as tic-tac-toe!)

875 AD: The Age of the Vikings

Viking fathers were often away on long voyages, so children had to help their mothers with chores such as raising the farm animals, harvesting crops of oats, barley, and cabbage, and stitching tunics and blankets made from wool.

Viking kids loved competitive sports, especially wrestling and swimming. In the evenings, they huddled around the fire and listened to stories of Norse giants and sea serpents. Girls learned not only how to cook, but also how to heal wounds with medicinal herbs and plants. They learned these skills when they were very young because most Viking girls were married by the age of thirteen!

1144 AD: The Middle Ages

Many peasant families sent their children to work instead of school. Children as young as five worked as servants in wealthy households. They would churn butter, collect eggs, scrub floors, and empty chamber pots. If his father was skilled, a boy could become an apprentice, learning a specific trade such as glove-making, carpentry, or blacksmithing.

Only children from noble families could enjoy board games like chess. However, peasant children did play games of dice (made from bones) and marbles (made from clay). Children sometimes played with wooden swords, but the nobles did not want peasant children to learn how to battle—they were worried that the peasants would one day overthrow their lords.

1600s: New World

Children who sailed across the Atlantic Ocean to live in the "New World" probably did not have much room to play in. The ship was cramped with sailors, passengers, barrels, supplies, and livestock. While onboard, kids helped by keeping things as clean as possible (which was not easy) in order to avoid disease.

During sunny days, children could be on deck in the fresh air. But when the winds shifted and storms began, they waited below deck, passing the time by singing and talking about their dreams of a new life in America.

1700s: Colonial America
In the 1700s, parents gave children their first pair of durable shoes at the age of six. After that, it was work, work, work! Children in rural communities helped their mothers milk cows and make candles. They assisted their fathers with shoeing horses and bailing hay. Children living in towns could help shopkeepers stock their shelves, bakers bake bread, and printers distribute pamphlets.

Kids still found time for fun, though. Boys and girls often built their own toys like stilts, popguns, and rocking horses. They played ball games such as ninepins (an early form of bowling) and rounders (an early form of baseball).

1800s: Pioneer Days
In the early 1800s, the United States began expanding its borders. Thousands of adventurous folks headed west, traveling in wagon trains pulled by oxen and mules. Pioneer children passed the time by singing prairie songs, playing with rag dolls, and whittling animals out of wood.

Once they arrived at their new settlement, there were lots of chores to do. Stacking firewood, plowing the fields, fishing for supper, and building fences were all ways for youngsters to pitch in.

1900s: The Turn of the Century
Just because many kids in the early 1900s lived in large cities didn't mean their lives were easy. Many homes did not have indoor plumbing, so boys and girls had to fetch water from a community water pump. Then, after lugging the water back home, they washed the dishes. After all of their chores were done, most children went to school. Sadly, many poor children left school early on to work in factories in order to help their families earn money.

Kids played lots of sports, including a game called stickball which could be played on just about any street or alleyway. Many girls focused on music, art, and decoration. But they also watched and encouraged their mothers as the women fought for the right to vote.

1950s: The Fabulous Fifties
There were a lot of "nifty" inventions to help kids with their chores in the 1950s. Many suburban households had automatic dishwashers, electric stoves, and motorized lawn mowers. Kids earned extra money by working paper routes or setting up their own lemonade stands.

Kids bounced on pogo sticks, gyrated with Hula-hoops, and zoomed on roller skates. And when they were done playing outside, they often read comic books or watched shows like *Howdy Doody* on the family's black-and-white television.

Present Day
Today, children still do many of the same chores they did hundreds of years ago: pulling weeds, helping with the laundry, cleaning around the house, and, of course, making their beds.

To Mom and Grandma. —W.B.
To Joseph, Tommy, and Jazzy. —J.V.

Text copyright © 2011 by Wade Bradford
Illustrations copyright © 2011 by Johanna van der Sterre

Library of Congress Cataloging-in-Publication Data

Bradford, Wade.
Why do I have to make my bed? / by Wade Bradford. —1st ed.
p. cm.
Summary: When a boy asks his mother why he must make his bed, she tells him a story about his ancestors who posed the same question through the centuries, going all the way back to a caveboy and his mother.
[1. Housekeeping—Fiction. 2. Mothers and son—Fiction.] I. Title.
PZ7.B7229Why 2011
[Fic]—dc22
2009045487

ISBN 978-1-58246-327-8 (hardcover)
ISBN 978-1-58246-388-9 (Gibraltar lib. bdg.)

Printed in China

Design by Melissa Brown
Typeset in Chop Phooey and Billy
The illustrations in this book were rendered in watercolor and digitally finished in Adobe Photoshop.

1 2 3 4 5 6 — 16 15 14 13 12 11

First Edition